Ebb and Flo
and the
New Friend

by Jane Simmons

Margaret K. McElderry Books

To Neil, who made it all possible. —J. S.

Margaret K. McElderry Books
An imprint of Simon & Schuster Children's Publishing Division
1230 Avenue of the Americas
New York, New York 10020

Copyright © 1998 by Jane Simmons

First published in Great Britain by Orchard Children's Books
First United States Edition, 1999
10 9 8 7 6 5 4 3 2 1
Printed in Singapore

Library of Congress Catalog Card Number: 98-87874
ISBN: 0-689-82483-1

Ebb sat in her favorite spot.
Things couldn't have been better.
Suddenly she heard a flapping noise
and was gently pushed by something soft and warm . . .

and there it sat: a bird, in Ebb's
favorite spot.

Flo giggled.

Beep, beep, beep, said the bird.

"Isn't she lovely, Ebb," said Flo. "She wants to be friends
with you."

Ebb growled.

Beep, beep, beep, said the bird.

That night Ebb did not sleep well.

As the days passed, Ebb got grumpier.
"Look at that bird! Isn't she sweet?"
people would say.
Beep, beep, beep, said the bird.
Grrr, grrr, Ebb growled.

Even Granny liked Bird and fed it Ebb's tidbits.
Beep, beep, beep, said the bird.
Ebb wished Bird would fly far away
and never come back.

The very next morning, Ebb's wish came true.
"Oh, no. Bird has gone!" cried Flo.

When they went out, Ebb had
her favorite spot all to herself.
Things couldn't have been better.

Only, she had to eat her dinner all by herself. It felt strange without Bird getting in the way.

And somehow she couldn't sleep very well, now that she was alone. It was too quiet without Bird's beeping, and her bed was too cold and empty.

Even at Granny's, all Ebb could think of was
Bird. She didn't want her tidbits. Ebb wasn't
happy at all.

As the long, hot summer days passed,
the dragonflies buzzed and the birds sang.
Ebb saw some geese on the river . . .

but none of them swam near
the boat.

"Come on, Ebb," said Flo.
"Let's go fishing."

But it was no good. Ebb
missed Bird more than ever.

Then one day, *Beep, beep, beep!* heard Ebb.
"Bird!" called Flo.
Ebb barked excitedly.

And there Bird sat in Ebb and
Bird's favorite spot.

Things couldn't have been better.